THE FOX

*went out on
a chilly night*

An Old Song
Illustrated by
PETER SPIER

DOUBLEDAY
NEW YORK   LONDON   TORONTO   SYDNEY   AUCKLAND

The fox went out on a chilly night,

and he prayed to the moon to give him light,

for he'd many miles to go that night

before he reached the town-o, town-o, town-o,

for he'd many miles to go that night

before he reached the town-o.

He ran till he came to the farmer's bin,

where the ducks and the geese were kept penned in.

"A couple of you will grease my chin

before I leave this town-o, town-o, town-o.

A couple of you will grease my chin

before I leave this town-o."

First he caught the grey goose by the neck,

then he swung a duck across his back.

And he didn't mind the quack, quack, quack,

or their legs all dangling down-o, down-o, down-o.

And he didn't mind the quack, quack, quack,

or their legs all dangling down-o.

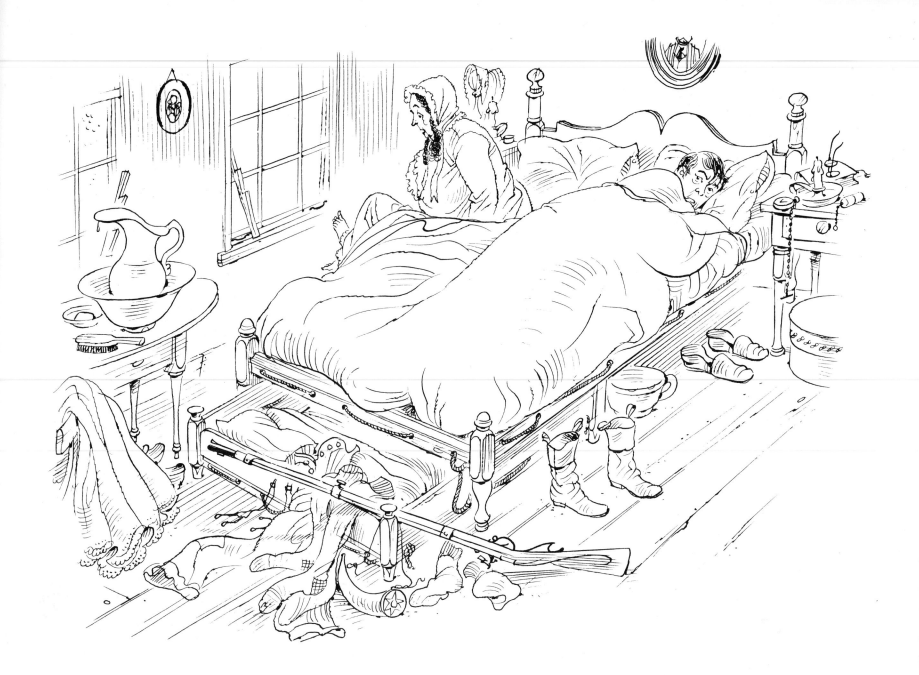

Then old mother Giggle-Gaggle jumped out of bed.

Out of the window she popped her head,

crying, "John! John! Our grey goose is gone,

and the fox is in the town-o, town-o, town-o,"

crying, "John! John! Our grey goose is gone

and the fox is in the town-o."

Then John, he ran to the top of the hill,

blew his horn both loud and shrill.

The fox, he said, "I better go with my kill

or they'll soon be on my tail-o, tail-o, tail-o."

The fox, he said, "I better go with my kill

or they'll soon be on my tail-o."

He ran till he came to his nice warm den.

There were the little ones, eight, nine, ten.

They said, "Daddy, better go back again,

because it must be a wonderful town-o, town-o, town-o."

Then the fox and his wife, without any strife,

cut up the goose with a fork and a knife.

They never ate such a dinner in their life

and the little ones chewed on the bones-o, bones-o, bones-o.

They never ate such a dinner in their life

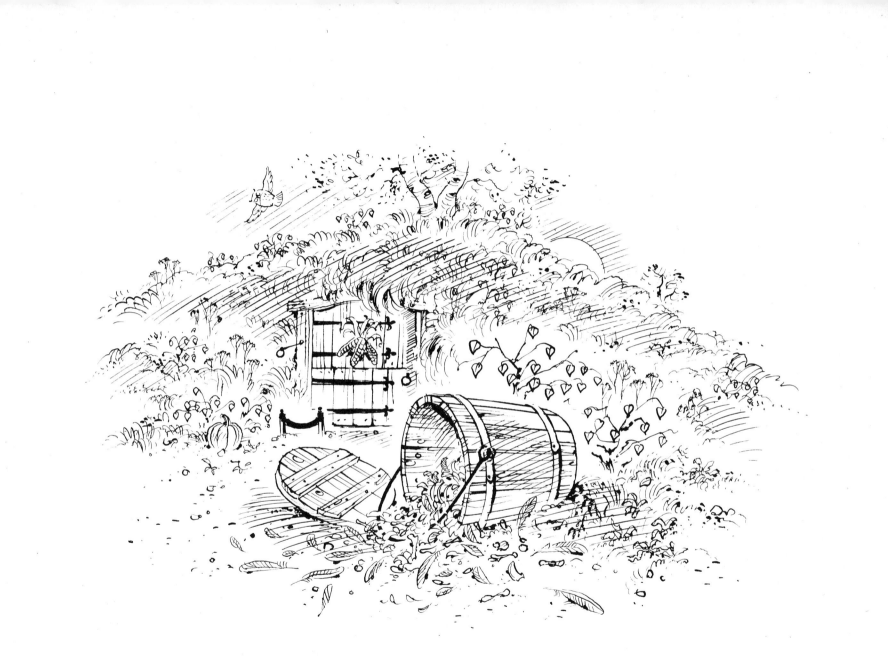

and the little ones chewed on the bones-o.

Lively.

1. The fox went out on a chil-ly night, and he town - o, town - o, town - o, for he'd man - y miles to

prayed to the moon to give him light, for he'd go that night be - fore he reached the

man - y miles to go that night be - fore he reached the town - o. 2. He